The Knightlands

HOWARD KENT

Paperback: 978-1-964035-46-8
eBook: 978-1-964035-47-5
Library of Congress Control Number: 2024921602

This is a work of nonfiction.

Table of Contents

Prologue

The night was cloaked in darkness and foreboding, heavy clouds hanging in the sky like ominous specters. A lone figure emerged from the shadows, shrouded in mystery and surrounded by the eerie sounds of the night. It was a priestess, her presence a beacon of light amidst the encroaching darkness.

As lightning streaked across the sky, illuminating the scene with its blinding flashes, a fearsome creature materialized before her eyes - a great red dragon. Its scales shimmered with an iridescent red hue, reflecting the ethereal glow of moonlight. The priestess felt her heart race as she stared into its piercing gaze.

Fear gripped her very being as she desperately tried to turn and flee to safety. But to her horror, she found that her feet were rooted to the ground as if held captive by some unseen force. She attempted to scream for help, but no sound escaped her lips. The dragon's presence seemed to steal away not only her voice but also her ability to move.

And then it happened – a terrifying sight that would forever haunt her dreams. The dragon opened its monstrous maw, revealing rows upon rows of razor-sharp teeth gleaming ominously in the dim light. Time seemed to stand still as an inferno roared forth from its gaping jaws.

Chapter 1

In the quiet solitude of her quarters, Elara Silvermist jolts awake, drenched in sweat, as her nightmare releases its grip on her. Gasping for breath, she tries to steady herself, but her racing heart refuses to calm down. Just as she begins to regain some semblance of composure, the door to her chamber bursts open, startling her even further.

Laura's attendant rushes into the room with concern etched across her face. "Is everything alright, Priestess? I heard a scream," she stammers out in a worried tone.

Elara brushes away the perspiration clinging to her forehead and offers her a weak smile. "Yes, yes. I am fine," she assures her. "I just need a moment to collect myself. You may return to your own sleeping chambers."

The attendant bows respectfully and retreats from the room without another word spoken. Left alone once more, Elara finds solace in gazing out of the window at the holy city sprawled below. The moon hangs full and radiant in the night sky, casting an ethereal glow over the surrounding countryside.

As Elara's gaze drifts across the landscape bathed in various shades of silver and gray, she spots scattered torchlights twinkling like distant fireflies against the darkness. It is a sight that brings both comfort and unease to her troubled mind.

"The high priests must be informed," Elara resolves silently within herself. "The forces of evil must not prevail." With renewed determination coursing through her veins, she readies herself for what lies ahead - a meeting with the high priests who hold sway over matters of great importance.

Clad in ceremonial robes befitting her esteemed position as priestess of light and truth, Elara makes her way through dimly lit corridors towards the sacred chamber where those entrusted with safeguarding ancient knowledge convene.

As she walks, memories of her upbringing in Valoria flood her thoughts. Born into a humble family, Elara had always possessed an innate sense of purpose and a deep connection to the spiritual realm. From a young age, she exhibited extraordinary abilities that set her apart from others - the gift of foresight and an unyielding determination to vanquish darkness.

It was this unwavering resolve that led her to be chosen as the High Priestess of Light, tasked with defending the realm against the encroaching forces of evil. Elara's heart swells with pride and trepidation at the weighty responsibility bestowed upon her shoulders.

As she approaches the grandiose doors leading to the chamber, Elara feels a mix of anticipation and anxiety knotting in her stomach. She takes a deep breath to steady herself before pushing open the doors, revealing a room bathed in soft light emanating from ornate candelabras lining its walls.

The high priests are gathered around an intricately carved table adorned with sacred artifacts - symbols of their authority and wisdom. Their eyes turn towards Elara as she enters, acknowledging her presence with respect and curiosity.

Elara takes her place at the head of the table, facing these venerable figures who hold immense power within their hands. The weight of their collective gaze bears down on her like an invisible force, but she does not waver.

With conviction in her voice, Elara recounts every harrowing detail of her nightmare - visions that portend great danger looming over their beloved land. She speaks fervently about dark omens and signs that cannot be ignored any longer.

The high priests listen intently, their expressions shifting from skepticism to concern as they absorb every word uttered by their chosen priestess. The gravity of Elara's words resonates within each soul present; it is undeniable that something sinister stirs on the horizon.

After what feels like an eternity of silence, the eldest high priest, his eyes filled with wisdom and sorrow, speaks in a voice that carries the weight of centuries. "Elara Silvermist, your vision is not to be taken lightly. The forces of darkness grow bolder with each passing day. We must act swiftly to preserve the light."

His words hang in the air, lingering like a solemn promise. Elara's heart quickens as she realizes that her calling goes beyond mere dreams and prophecies - it is a summons to rise above herself and lead her people towards salvation.

With renewed determination burning in her eyes, Elara nods solemnly. "I am prepared to face whatever trials lay before us," she declares resolutely. "For I am the bearer of light and the protector of world Zemlundia.»

The sun rose over the "garden of serenity," casting a gentle glow on Elara, who sat in the middle of the chapel garden, engrossed in her ancient texts and scrolls. As she delved into the wisdom of ages past, her personal attendant, Belinda, approached and took a seat beside her.

"Hello, priestess. How are you this morning?" Belinda greeted with a warm smile.

Elara looked up from her reading and returned the smile. "I am fine, Belinda. I am simply enjoying the sunlight before embarking on my journey."

Belinda hesitated for a moment before speaking softly. "Pardon me for asking, priestess, but... about last night. Your dreams..."

Elara's gaze shifted to her scrolls as she pondered Belinda's question. "My dreams have become increasingly violent. Is that what you wanted to know?"

Blushing with embarrassment, Belinda quickly replied, "I didn't mean to pry."

Placing a reassuring hand on Belinda's arm, Elara said gently, "No need to be embarrassed; I appreciate your concern."

A spark of relief lit up Belinda's eyes as she smiled back at Elara. "I am always here for you, priestess. Do you wish to talk about your nightmares?"

Elara nodded thoughtfully. "Yes, you're right, Belinda. Talking about it might offer some clarity and provide a fresh perspective." She took a deep breath before continuing.

"For the past two seasons," Elara began slowly, "I have been plagued by horrific visions and nightmares—dark omens that grow stronger with each passing night." She paused briefly before adding with intensity in her voice: "But last night was different; it felt personal—almost as if it was directed at me!"

Belinda's face grew serious as she listened attentively. "What do you believe these dreams signify, priestess?"

Elara locked eyes with Belinda, her gaze unwavering. "I believe they foretell a great peril approaching—a threat so immense that it could bring devastation to our lands."

Belinda's concern deepened. "And what must be done, priestess?"

Elara's voice resonated with conviction as she answered, "To halt the advancing threat of the great dragon."

Chapter 2

The sun shone brightly as three women made their way towards an outside spring, carrying their water buckets. They walked leisurely, unaware of the twelve pairs of eyes watching them from the surrounding brush. Six goblins, with warts covering their faces and short swords in hand, waited for the perfect moment to attack.

As the women finished filling their buckets, one of them thought she heard a rustling sound coming from the underbrush. Another lady paused as she heard something snap in the bushes. Suddenly, a rusty throwing knife sprang from the bush and lodged itself into the back of one woman's right leg. She let out a scream as she felt the cold metal piercing her skin.

The six goblins approached and encircled the terrified women, baring their teeth menacingly. "Goblins! We are surrounded!" cried out one of the ladies as another rushed to comfort her injured companion. "Leave us alone!"

Just when it seemed like all hope was lost, a crossbow bolt pierced through one of the goblins' chests, sending it flying backward. The remaining goblins looked down at their fallen comrade only to find themselves face-to-face with a large humanoid figure clad in full plate armor and holding a crossbow.

Recognizing his attire as that of a holy knight from the church by his tunic, which was adorned with a red lion on its white chest-plate cloth, relief washed over the ladies' faces. The knight moved purposefully to stand between them and their attackers while setting aside his crossbow to draw his two-handed sword.

With authority in his voice, he shouted at the goblins, "Be gone! You have no business being here!"

Realizing they were facing formidable opposition, moments passed before hesitation filled their beady eyes. Slowly but surely, they turned tail and fled into the safety of trees lining the forest.

Feeling secure in the situation, the knight sheathed his sword and knelt beside the injured woman. His keen eyes noticed that her skin had changed to a different hue than her companions, indicating a possible poisoning. "We have to get her to the church immediately," he said with urgency in his voice.

Before he could make any further moves, a familiar melodic voice spoke from behind him. It was Elara Silvermist, clad in her priestess robes. "There will be no need for that, sir knight," she said softly.

Thane Brightshield, as the knight was called, smiled broadly at Elara's timely arrival. "You couldn't have come at a better time."

Elara examined the injured woman and placed her hands on her leg as she began to pray to the 'Ancient of Days.' A white light suddenly enveloped the wounded woman's body, and miraculously, her wound began closing up before their eyes. The injured woman slowly opened her eyes and smiled as she realized she was free from pain. "Thank you, priestess! Thank you so much!"

Elara humbly replied with a warm smile, "Don't thank me; thank the Creator who loves you."

With their immediate danger resolved, the women gathered their water containers and hurried back towards the city while Thane took a moment to sit against a nearby tree and examine his shoulder wound. Elara joined him under the shade of the tree.

"What am I going to do with you?" Elara smirked.

Thane looked up at her and returned her smile. "Don't worry about me; I've dealt with worse."

Elara noticed Thane rubbing his shoulder then helped him remove his shoulder plate gently before examining his discomfort more closely. Without waiting for permission from Thane, she placed her hands just above it and summoned a small glowing sphere of light that surrounded his shoulder. "It should feel better soon," she reassured him.

Curiosity sparked in her eyes as she asked, "So, it like you injured your shoulder my brave and fearless knight?"

Thane glanced back at her with a hint of amusement. "And why are you out here without your escort, Elara?"

The priestess giggled softly. "I asked you first."

Thane rubbed his shoulder and noticed that it was no longer sore. "Well... truth be known, I was on my way to meet with you. I heard a woman's scream as I approached the 'Garden of Serenity.' I didn't expect to be fighting off a group of wild goblins."

Elara furrowed her eyebrows slightly. "I thought goblins were creatures of the night?"

"So did I," Thane replied with concern evident in his voice. "Things are changing in this world, and I'm trying to make sense of it all."

The knight and the priestess then rose to their feet. Thane gestured towards the direction of the church, offering his escort services to Elara.

Grateful for his chivalry, Elara bowed respectfully. "Why thank you, sir knight."

And so, as they had done for many seasons before, Thane and Elara walked back towards the church.

Chapter 3

Elara Silvermist stood in the middle of a round courtroom, surrounded by high arches and multiple seats on different levels. The room belonged to the high elders of 'The Church of the Living Son.' Elara couldn't believe what she was hearing. Just moments ago, the elders had given their approval for her to leave, but now High Elder Ramus was countermanding their decision.

Frustration boiled within Elara as High Elder Ramus slammed his fist onto the desk in front of him. "No! We cannot allow you to leave!" His voice echoed through the room, filled with authority.

Determined not to back down, Elara squared her shoulders and met Ramus's gaze. "I have seen a great threat in my visions," she declared firmly.

Ramus adjusted his robes, standing tall and confident. "I have not felt this threat that you claim to have seen," he retorted dismissively.

Elara's eyes widened in disbelief. "Then how do you explain the goblins attacking our water-bearers in broad daylight? This is no mere coincidence!"

Ramus glanced around at the other elders before crossing his arms over his chest. "That may be strange indeed, but it is not relevant to our discussion," he stated coldly. "We require your presence here, fulfilling your duties within these walls."

The fire within Elara burned brighter as she raised her voice. "This concerns all of us, great elders! If we fail to find and eradicate this growing evil, it could endanger every soul in this region."

Ramus's annoyance was evident on his face as he replied with a hint of arrogance, "There is no evil that our holy knights cannot handle within these walls."

"But High Elder Ramus!" Elara pleaded desperately. "I implore you to listen-"

Ramus swiftly raised his hand to silence her. "This discussion is over," he declared firmly, his voice leaving no room for further argument.

Feeling defeated but not willing to give up, Elara folded her robes tightly around her and took a deep breath. "Fine!" she exclaimed, her voice filled with defiance. "But let it be known that I protest this decision, great elders." With those words, she turned and stormed out of the courtroom.

As Elara made her way through the dimly lit corridors of the church, anger coursed through her veins. How could they dismiss the very real danger she had seen in her visions? She knew she had to take matters into her own hands.

As the sun began to set on the little village of Greenhaven, two figures walked along the roadside towards the entrance of a tavern called 'The Red Griffin Inn'. The taller figure, a strikingly handsome man with sandy blonde hair and royal green and brown robes, opened the door for his female companion. She wore studded leather armor and carried weapons at her side.

Inside the dimly lit tavern, they found an open table near the flickering fireplace. The inn was bustling with activity. The man, named Kael, smiled at his companion and asked her what she would like to drink. Lila responded with her usual rye remark and requested a Suz-ale.

Kael signaled a busty waitress over to their table who flirtatiously approached them. They ordered two Suz-ales but were offered cheap beer instead. Lila gave Kael an icy stare as he blushed in response and declined the offer.

Curious about their presence in Greenhaven, Lila questioned Kael's decision to come to this backwater town. He explained that they needed some rest after escorting a Duke's son who proved to be quite demanding.

Their conversation was interrupted by a panicked young man bursting into the inn warning everyone about approaching goblins. However, he was met with skepticism from both patrons and the innkeeper who argued that goblins did not come out in daylight.

As tensions rose between them, Kael suggested that investigating this matter might be worthwhile. Lila disagreed, emphasizing that they wouldn't be paid for it and it should be left for the villagers to handle.

Undeterred by Lila's reluctance, Kael hinted at a potential reward for saving the village from goblin attacks. This sparked Lila's interest but she remained skeptical about whether there would actually be any reward at all.

They continued their silent standoff until Kael leaned back slightly in his chair and took another sip of his drink, maintaining eye contact with Lila. She defiantly stared back, refusing to be swayed.

The innkeeper eventually restored order and instructed everyone to enjoy the hospitality of The Red Griffin Inn. The musicians resumed playing their tunes, creating a lively atmosphere.

Kael and Lila continued to observe the scene around them, contemplating their next move. The possibility of a reward still lingered in Kael's mind, while Lila remained cautious about involving themselves in the village's problems without any guaranteed compensation.

As they sat there in silence, weighing their options, a thought occurred to Kael. He leaned forward and whispered to Lila, "Don't look at me like that... What if we do this for our own sake? To prove our worth as heroes?"

Lila raised an eyebrow but said nothing. She knew that Kael had a point - sometimes it wasn't about the money or recognition; it was about doing what was right and making a difference in the world.

Later that evening, in the tranquil ambiance of "The Hall of the Sacred Scrolls," Elara sat in the grand study hall, a quill in hand. She was engrossed in her studies when frustration overcame her, causing her to throw the quill down onto the parchment.

Thane, ever vigilant as her personal protector, noticed Elara's discontent and spoke to her in a soft and reassuring voice. "Are you okay, m'lady?"

Elara looked up at Thane with weary eyes. "No, I'm not. I'm absolutely furious. I cannot comprehend the decision made by the high elders. How dare they ignore the facts I presented? They wouldn't even let me finish speaking."

She placed her head between her hands, a gesture revealing both frustration and sadness. "Don't they care? Doesn't the church have a duty and responsibility to protect its citizens from any potential threat? It truly saddens me."

Elara sighed deeply before continuing with a heavy heart. "If something isn't done soon, those blessings that we hold so dear will be lost forever. The great dragon will devour those who remain oblivious to his presence."

Thane gently placed his hand on Elara's shoulder, offering comfort and support. "Is there anything I can do to help? Perhaps make an inquiry on your behalf?"

Elara reached out and touched Thane's hand affectionately before leaning her head against it for solace. "You're very kind, Thane, but if the elders refuse to take action despite this dire situation, then it falls upon me alone. How can I turn away from this calling placed within my heart by none other than the 'Ancient of Days' himself?"

Thane took a deep breath and responded with unwavering conviction in his voice. "I would say that it would be nothing short of a sin to disregard a request from the creator of this vast universe."

Elara's head lowered, contemplating Thane's words. "I need to pray. I must seek guidance to navigate the tumultuous emotions that consume me."

With that, Elara began to pray fervently. Thane resumed his position as her unwavering protector, standing guard over the delicate figure of the priestess.

Minutes passed in quiet reverence as Elara remained deep in prayer. Suddenly, a faint rustling outside the doorway caught Thane's attention. The doors opened slowly, and a small attendant timidly entered the room. The sound of the entrance reverberated within the sacred hall, drawing Elara's gaze towards him.

Recognizing the priestess, the attendant bowed respectfully before addressing them in a soft and timid voice. "M'lady, M'lord, I apologize for disturbing you. High Elder Ramus requests your presence in the garden of serenity."

Thane and Elara exchanged shocked glances at each other before rising from their seats with purposeful determination.

High Elder Ramus rarely summoned anyone to such a tranquil place unless grave matters weighed heavy on his mind. Feeling an undeniable sense of urgency surging through their veins, they followed without hesitation.

As they made their way through dimly lit corridors towards the garden of serenity, Elara couldn't help but feel an overwhelming sense of responsibility weighing upon her shoulders. She knew that she alone held the key to unlocking their future and protecting those who depended on her wisdom and guidance.

The moon cast its gentle glow upon them as they stepped into the serene garden filled with fragrant blossoms and calming fountains. High Elder Ramus awaited them beneath an ancient tree whose branches seemed to reach towards heaven itself.

His eyes held both weariness and determination as he addressed them solemnly. "Elara, Thane... we stand at a precipice where our decisions will shape the destiny of our land. The time has come for you, Elara, to embrace the weight of your divine calling and lead our people towards salvation."

Before Elara could utter a single word, High Elder Ramus raised his hand, silencing her. "I do want to apologize for this morning's proceedings. After careful consideration, I believe there may be some truth in what you presented," he admitted.

Elara gazed at the high elder with a mix of curiosity and skepticism. Sensing her reaction, Ramus continued, "I'll keep it brief. Four days ago, we dispatched one of our most trusted scribes and a knight to an abandoned castle on our border. Since then, we've received no word from them."

Ramus glanced sideways at Elara before posing a question. "Have you ever heard of the holy stone?"

"Yes," Elara responded cautiously, "but it was always considered a mere legend. There is no mention of it in the sacred texts."

"Indeed," Ramus acknowledged with intertwined fingers resting pensively under his chin. "The stone's existence is not mentioned in the texts, but I assure you that it is real."

"The holy stone is an extraordinary artifact," he continued. "It was entrusted to our ancestors when the 'Ancient of Days' walked among us humans. Its power was so immense that it had to be hidden away and guarded for thousands of years."

"When the 'Ancient of Days' sacrificed himself to save us from the dragon menace, the stone shattered into several shards—each possessing its own divine power." Ramus paused briefly before continuing.

"For decades now, these shards have been sought after by many but never found." His gaze shifted between Elara and Thane.

"After consulting with some of my fellow high elders through prayer," Ramus announced gravely, "we have come to believe that both you and Thane should lead this investigation."

Elara could hardly believe what she was hearing; she was dumbfounded by this unexpected turn of events. It was highly unusual for her and Ramus to see eye to eye on anything. As she processed the gravity of the situation, Elara noticed Ramus shifting his attention towards Thane.

"Thane Brightshield," Ramus declared authoritatively, "you have been entrusted with the task of protecting High Priestess Elara Silvermist in her quest to locate these shards and prevent impending evil. Do you understand?"

Thane stood tall and resolute. "Completely, High Elder."

Ramus briefly lowered his head, walking past both the high priestess and the holy knight. However, he suddenly halted and turned around to face them once more. "I request your presence in my chambers tomorrow morning. There, you will receive your first duty," he said solemnly before departing.

As Ramus began walking away, Thane leaned closer to Elara's ear and whispered softly, "Looks like your prayers have been answered."

Elara's mind was a whirlwind of thoughts as she tried to comprehend what lay ahead for them both. This unexpected mission not only challenged her beliefs but also thrust her into an alliance with Thane—a man she barely knew but now relied upon deeply.

The weight of responsibility settled upon their shoulders as they contemplated the magnitude of their task: finding the shattered shards of the holy stone before it fell into malevolent hands.

The sun began its descent beyond the horizon as Elara and Thane walked side by side towards their respective quarters in preparation for what awaited them on this perilous journey.

Chapter 4

The 'Tavern of the Morning Star' was abuzz with activity. The air was thick with the scent of cooked meat and garlic potatoes, while lively tunes played by musicians filled the room. Thane Brightshield, the legendary holy knight of Valoria, sat at a table, sipping his drink amidst the merriment.

For hours, Thane had been unable to sleep after his meeting with High Elder Ramus. His mind was filled with questions and uncertainties about what lay ahead. As he sat lost in thought, the tavern door swung open once again, revealing Elara entering with two unfamiliar figures in tow.

Elara spotted Thane and made her way towards him through the crowded tavern. Concern etched on her face, she asked, "I thought I'd find you here. Is everything okay?"

Thane looked into his mug without answering for a moment before finally responding, "I don't know. It's just a feeling I've got. Like something's about to happen, but I don't know what."

A friendly waitress approached their table and addressed Elara politely, "Hello, M'lady. Can I get you anything to drink?"

Elara smiled warmly and replied, "Tea would be fine though I can't stay very long. I have to get back to the church and finish a few personal chores before my meeting with the high elders."

The barmaid reassured her saying it wouldn't take long as she headed towards the kitchen.

Elara took a seat beside Thane and asked him curiously,"So what are you drinking?"

Thane smiled as he held up his mug,"Some spiced cider. It's been my favorite since I was a child." He then turned his attention back to Elara,"By the way, what are you doing here?"

Worry evident in her eyes as she stared at him intently, Elara replied,"I was just worried about you. And I wanted to say thank you for being there for me. I couldn't ask for anybody else to have by my side."

A faint blush colored Thane's cheeks as he responded,"I am very flattered." His expression then turned serious,"But I hope you know that what we are about to do isn't a game. If this calling is from the 'Ancient of Days', you know it won't be easy."

Elara's tone matched his seriousness as she replied,"Oh believe me, Thane, I know. I am somewhat frightened by the prospect of leaving home for days at a time in a land that has been so corrupted and dangerous. But there are people who need to know the truth."

Thane nodded solemnly, understanding the weight of her conviction and the immense pressure she must be under.

Just then, their conversation was changed when the knight asked her who the two strangers were that she walked in with. As the barmaid delivered her tea, Elara explained. "I saw these two wandering alone just outside of town. They were looking for a place to stay, so I directed them here." She gestured towards the tall figure in green robes with an oaken staff and the attractive woman with long curly blonde hair dressed in leather armor.

As he observed them from across the room, Thane commented,"Well, it looks like you made a good decision bringing them somewhere safe. I just hope they're not here to start trouble because I would sure hate to have to take newcomers in and throw them in the dungeon."

Elara stood up abruptly realizing she needed to leave soon,"I must take my leave of you, Sir Knight." Thane also rose from his seat,"Will I see you tomorrow?"

He bowed respectfully,"I give you my word, High Priestess."

Before either could make another move, a loud crash erupted from a nearby table. A large man was gripping a small boy tightly, anger etched on his face. Thane's instincts kicked in, and he swiftly made his way towards the commotion.

In a commanding voice, Thane spoke,"Faldon! Steel yourself! You're making a big mistake if you think you're going to abuse that child!"

Faldon, the heavyset man, gave Thane a disgusted look,"This doesn't concern you, knight. I have personal business to deal with this little punk!"

Thane's hand tightened around the hilt of his sword,"Faldon! If that boy has one hand struck against him, it will be lying on the ground next to your head!"

Reluctantly releasing the young boy from his grip, Faldon sneered,"Fine! But mark my words, knight. This isn't over!»

As the situation seemed to defuse for a moment, a melodious voice broke through the tension,"If you don't go with that knight, then you're going to deal with me!"

All eyes turned towards Lila as she stood her ground. Faldon laughed mockingly at her,"Hah! You?! A girl?"

Unfazed by his taunts, Lila retorted confidently,"You owe my companion and me another drink! That poor boy you threw landed on our table. So what's it going to be?"

Faldon's anger grew as he postured like an attacking bear,"Woman! Don't you know who you're talking to?"

Lila smirked mischievously as she placed her hands on her hips,"Nobody important I would say."

Enraged now, Faldon drew his sword and threatened Lila while boasting about his strength. However, before he could make a move towards her, Kael stepped forward and whispered an incantation under his breath,"For those that walk, to those that creep. Make this brute fall dead asleep!"

A shimmering, sparkling gold light surrounded Faldon's eyes momentarily before he collapsed onto the floor, fast asleep.

At that moment, city guards arrived on the scene. Elara pointed them towards the slumbering Faldon and Thane stepped forward,"Place him under arrest. I believe a short stay in the dungeon should help his demeanor somewhat."

The guards acted swiftly, removing Faldon from the tavern as Thane turned his attention to the young boy who had been at the center of it all. The boy approached Elara and Thane with an apologetic look on his face,"I am so sorry I caused all this trouble, but I wanted to say thank you."

Thane's voice softened as he reassured him,"It's okay, son." He reached into his pouch and handed him some gold pieces,"Why don't you go home and help feed your family?"

Gratefulness filled the young boy's eyes as he bowed respectfully before running out of the tavern. Elara smiled affectionately at Thane,"You continue to impress me every single time. You'd think I should be used to this by now."

A small chuckle escaped Thane's lips,"Nothing makes me laugh more than seeing the wind knocked out of a blowhard. I really thought I was going to have to fight that brute for a moment."

Elara then turned her attention back to Lila and Kael,"On behalf of the church, I want to thank you for standing up against what was clearly an injustice."

Lila responded with a smirk,"You're welcome, Priestess. But in truth, it's hard for me to restrain myself when I come across people who think they are in control. Sometimes I just get bored."

Kael leaned on his staff thoughtfully,"Sometimes there is too little excitement in life not to do anything."

Elara introduced them formally to Thane,"Now if you will excuse me, I have to get back to the church. Sir Knight, would you be available to accompany me?"

Thane nodded in agreement as they made their way towards the tavern doors. Lila turned to Kael and asked,"Well... Do we stay here or do we continue on?"

Kael leaned on his staff and replied with a mysterious smile,"I believe those two have the answers we are looking for. I can't fully explain as of yet, but I think our reason for being here is not an accident."

The morning sun shone through the stained glass windows, casting colorful patterns on the exquisite chambers of High Elder Ramus. Thane and Elara stood before him, dressed in their finest attire, ready to embark on a dangerous mission. Ramus adjusted his regal robes and faced his two visitors with a solemn expression.

"I wanted to thank you both for coming," Ramus began, his voice filled with gravitas. "I wanted to press upon you the severity of what you will be entangled in."

Thane and Elara exchanged a glance, their determination unwavering. They knew that their journey would not be easy, but they were willing to face any challenge to protect their realm.

"There are a total of six shards that make up the holy stone," Ramus continued, his tone grave. "Each shard possesses great power and destructive potential."

He paused for a moment, allowing his words to sink in before continuing. "The shards hold immense power individually. However, the more they are used, the stronger their bond with their owner becomes. This bond can lead to dependence and eventually madness."

Thane furrowed his brow as he processed this information. The stakes were higher than he had initially anticipated. The fate of not only themselves but also everyone in the realm rested upon their success.

Ramus leaned forward slightly and fixed his gaze upon them intently. "Now regarding the value of these shards... How much do you think your lives are worth? If these shards fall into evil hands, it will bring death and slavery upon us all."

Elara felt a chill run down her spine at Ramus' words but refused to let fear cloud her judgment. She knew that they had been chosen for this quest because they possessed both strength and courage.

"We believe we know the location of one of the shards," Ramus said as he handed Elara a rolled piece of parchment. "Here's a map with markings indicating the possible last known location. Be careful, Elara."

Elara accepted the map with a determined nod. The weight of responsibility settled upon her shoulders, but she was ready to face whatever challenges lay ahead. Thane stood by her side, his unwavering loyalty evident in his eyes.

"We will do our best, High Elder," Elara said firmly, her voice filled with determination.

As Thane and Elara left High Elder Ramus' chambers, a small grin appeared on his face.

The sun began to set behind the white jagged mountains, casting a warm glow over the landscape as Thane and Elara rode on horseback. High Elder Ramus had provided them with directions, and they followed the dirt road, guided by the gentle breeze and rustling leaves. Elara was deeply engrossed in a leather brown book, her eyes scanning its pages as they continued their journey.

Thane glanced at Elara beside him and noticed her silence. "Elara, we've been riding all afternoon, and you haven't said a word. That must be quite an interesting book," he remarked curiously.

Elara smiled warmly at Thane. "I apologize for my silence, Thane. I've been studying the notes and information about the shards and the holy Stone mentioned in this book," she explained.

Intrigued, Thane asked, "Does it say anything about what these shards look like?"

Elara nodded and turned back to her book. "Indeed it does," she replied. "There's a sketch rendering here that describes them as approximately a hand span long with eight sides. They possess a deep richness in color and are said to be as hard as granite but as clean as lightning." She paused for effect before continuing solemnly, "When brought together, they mold into the holy stone itself. Each shard contains an indescribable power."

Impressed by this information, Thane let out a low whistle. "That's quite remarkable."

Elara's expression turned serious as she shared another important detail from the book's warning section. "However," she cautioned, "'Beware mortal,' it says here," she quoted from memory while making sure to emphasize each word clearly in her recitation of cautionary words.

"'For the shard you hold is a fragment of raw holiness,'" Elara continued dramatically. "'Imbued with the essence of the Ancient of Days. Its power is tantalizing, but its wrath is unforgiving. Those who dare to wield it without reverence and caution shall suffer the consequences of their arrogance. The shard will not be tamed, and its fury shall unleash a maelstrom of destruction upon the unwary. Handle it with reverence, lest you suffer the fate of those who have foolishly proceeded before you.'"

Thane's eyes widened in disbelief as he absorbed the weight of those words. "That sounds truly formidable," he remarked, shaking his head in awe. "I suppose High Elder Ramus was right to warn us about its power."

Elara nodded gravely in agreement. "Indeed, Thane," she said softly, "and I fear that this mission will be far more challenging than we anticipated."

Before Elara could finish her thought, a sudden blinding flash of light engulfed them both, momentarily blinding them and startling their horses into whinnying and bucking.

As their vision gradually returned to normal, Thane and Elara found themselves face-to-face with two figures standing in the middle of the road: Kael the Wizard and Lila the Rogue.

Kael stepped forward, his voice calm yet filled with urgency. "We apologize for our sudden appearance," he began courteously. "My comrade and I have been searching for you tirelessly. We are relieved to have finally found you."

Thane maneuvered his horse closer to Kael and regarded him cautiously. "You've caught me at a disadvantage," he admitted with a hint of suspicion in his voice. "What is it that you need from us?"

Kael exchanged a quick glance with Lila before turning back to Thane earnestly. "May we join your quest?" he asked sincerely. "We believe that our unique set of skills could greatly benefit you on this mission."

Thane glanced back at Elara, who nodded in agreement. He then looked back at Kael and Lila, his tone serious as he laid down the ground rules. "Very well," Thane agreed reluctantly.

"You may accompany us on this quest, but I must impress upon both of you that this is no mere field trip.Our mission is of utmost importance and delicate in nature."

Thane's eyes narrowed as he delivered his final instruction. "And one more thing," he added firmly, "you will follow my orders without question or hesitation. Is that understood?"

Lila grinned mischievously while Kael nodded respectfully. "So what are we waiting for?" Lila chimed in eagerly.

Chapter 5

Hours had passed since the four adventurers began their journey, and finally, they found themselves at the bottom of a massive stone stairway. Covered in cracks and overgrown with ivy, the stairway seemed to lead up to an ancient castle perched on top of a hill. As they gazed up at the castle, a full moon began its ascent behind it.

Lila gracefully slipped off the back of the horse she had been riding with Elara, her eyes fixed on the castle before them. "Well," she said with determination, "there's the castle."

Thane surveyed their surroundings and nodded in agreement. "It does appear as though it has been abandoned for years. It seems we'll have to climb from here."

Kael joined them by sliding off the back of his horse behind Thane. "Indeed, you are correct, Sir Knight," he replied solemnly. "This castle has been vacant for a very long time."

Elara raised an eyebrow inquisitively at Kael's statement. "It sounds like you know more about this place than you're letting on."

Kael turned his gaze towards Elara before returning his attention to the imposing structure ahead. "You are right, Priestess," he admitted reluctantly. "About a century ago, this castle was under the rule of King Grahame. He was a good and honorable man who governed with compassion and mercy." Kael paused briefly before continuing.

"He was also rumored to be one of the guardians of the shards you seek." The weight of his words hung heavily in the air.

Curiosity piqued within Elara as she absorbed this newfound information. "What happened here? Why is it abandoned?"

Kael's eyes grew distant as memories flooded back to him. "One day, without warning, a renegade ogre named Thunderstrike attacked this castle with an army of orcs and goblins. His sole intention was to possess the shard and gain unimaginable power."

"Grahame's troops fought valiantly," Kael continued, "but wave after wave of orcs broke through the king's defenses, overwhelming his soldiers with their sheer numbers."

Realization dawned on Elara as she grasped the gravity of the situation. "So, in order to protect the shard, King Grahame and a priest of light hid it within these very walls. Thunderstrike and his army have been searching for it ever since."

A flicker of unease crossed Lila's face as she interjected, "Let's hope that this ogre has either left or met his demise by now."

Elara nodded in agreement but felt a sense of urgency creeping into her bones. "Enough talk then," she said firmly. "It is time to start climbing. I do not wish to become a permanent fixture out here."

With renewed determination, they began their ascent up the weathered stone stairway. Each step brought them closer to their goal but also heightened the suspense that hung heavy in the air.

The castle stood before them, a haunting reminder of its former glory. Its once majestic spires and towers were now covered in ivy and moss, bearing the scars of time and neglect. The grand entrance, hidden behind overgrown brambles and vines, had lost its ornate carvings and intricate ironwork. The windows stared out like empty eyes, their shutters hanging askew or torn away altogether.

After a strenuous climb to the top, Elara was out of breath while Thane seemed unfazed. "That felt good to stretch my legs," Thane chuckled.

Elara gasped for air between words. "Thane... climbing up an entire side of a mountain... short climb to you?"

Thane continued to laugh as Elara regained her breath and approached the large oaken doors of the castle. Lila was already examining them closely.

"There don't seem to be any locks or obstacles," Lila said confidently. "It should be safe to proceed."

Thane stepped forward and placed his hands against the door. "Alright ladies, stand aside."

The doors resisted at first but with Thane's persistent effort, they started to give way until they splintered open.

As their eyes adjusted to the darkness inside, they found themselves in a dark and damp hallway. Once-bright torches now hung motionless on the walls.

Thane reached into his pouch and retrieved a tinder box containing flint and steel. He lit one of the torches from the wall, illuminating their path as they moved forward.

After walking about 50 feet down the hallway, they encountered a large pit stretching across it with three doors on each side overlooking it. Peering into its depths revealed only darkness.

Lila shook her head in response to Kael's question about its depth. "It's too dark down there; we can't tell. Perhaps it's magical, an illusion even. We shouldn't risk stepping off."

Elara nodded in agreement. "I wouldn't try either."

Kael rummaged through his backpack and pulled out a small, clear marble. He blew on it gently, and the orb began to glow as if it were daylight. "There, a simple solution."

Standing at the edge of the pit, Kael dropped the glowing orb down. It fell for a short time before bouncing off something large and disappearing into the water below.

Lila's eyes widened in surprise. "Did you see that? Something big is moving down there."

Thane estimated the depth of the pit to be around 100 feet. Elara looked at him with concern and asked how they would cross to reach the doors on the other side.

Lila smiled confidently as she pointed her torch towards the ceiling. "See those rungs up there? I have a rope we can tie around ourselves and swing across safely using them."

Elara gave Lila a skeptical look. "You may have the skills for that, but I fear the rest of us would end up as dinner for whatever lurks at the bottom of this pit."

Lila remained undeterred. "That's why we'll use this rope to secure ourselves while we swing across." She demonstrated by throwing a metal ring attached to one end of the rope through one of the rungs on the ceiling.

Lila then fastened both ends of the rope around her waist before swinging across with ease and catching onto a loose section of wall near two false doors that promptly fell into oblivion.

She grinned triumphantly. "Looks like we know which door to go through now."

Ensuring that it was unlocked, Lila opened it and made her way inside before tossing one end of the rope back across to Thane.

Thane secured himself with the rope and swung across to the safety of the other side. Elara turned to Kael, giving him a warm smile. "Well, it seems to be just the two of us left."

Kael handed her the rope. "I'll remain here, priestess. You go next."

Elara swung across and was caught by Thane on the other side. Before Thane could throw the rope back to Kael, he realized that the wizard had disappeared.

Thane panicked and called out his name, searching both sides of the pit and even peering into its darkness.

Suddenly, Kael's familiar voice came from behind him. "Do not fear, sir knight, for I am unharmed." It was Kael.

Stammering in disbelief, Thane asked how he had teleported to safety.

Kael smiled and explained his teleportation spell casually. Impressed by his magic skills, Thane suggested they keep moving forward.

In the dimly lit private study of high elder Ramus, the flickering shadows danced across the room as he sat at his desk, engrossed in a book. The soft glow from various candles cast an eerie ambiance, creating an atmosphere befitting the dark secrets that were harbored within those walls. Suddenly, a knock at his chamber door interrupted his reading.

"Come in!" Ramus called out, setting his book aside and preparing himself for whatever news awaited him.

As the heavy wooden door creaked open, a figure cloaked in deep red stepped into the room. The hood covered their face, making it impossible to discern their identity or intentions. Ramus peered intently at the mysterious visitor and gestured for them to speak.

"So..." Ramus began cautiously. "What news do you have for me?"

The stranger's voice resonated with a deep and menacing tone as they responded. "Priestess Elara has reached the castle, my Lord."

A sly smile crept across Ramus' face upon hearing this information. "Good," he said with satisfaction. "And am I to understand that her knight is still by her side?"

The hooded figure nodded silently before voicing their concerns. "Yes, my lord. However, there may be a problem."

Ramus arched an eyebrow curiously and leaned forward in his chair. "A problem? Pray tell."

"They seem to have acquired two additional adventurers during their journey," explained the stranger hesitantly. "Our spies do not recognize them."

Ramus scoffed dismissively at this revelation. "Bah! I'm not concerned about two more mere peasants meddling in our affairs. That castle will prove to be their downfall."

Curiosity getting the better of him, the hooded figure dared to ask further questions about Priestess Elara's significance in their plans. "May I ask, my lord, what is so important about this priestess that you wish her disposed of?"

Ramus took a moment to compose himself, his eyes narrowing with a mixture of annoyance and frustration. "Priestess Elara is a thorn in my side," he confessed bitterly. "For years, she has disrupted the natural order of things within our church."

His voice filled with disdain for the priestess's ideals, Ramus continued his tirade. "She believes that we should pay out money to these peasants who choose to remain in poverty. She fails to understand that their predicament is self-inflicted."

With a disdainful wave of his hand, Ramus revealed another layer to his motives. "That's precisely why we sent that inept scribe and his knight on the perilous mission to find the shard. They too had received visions similar to Elara's."

Ramus shook his head with a mixture of amusement and annoyance. "But no matter now. That simpleminded ogre Thunderstrike seems to be doing his job well enough, keeping those meddling fools away from our true purpose."

As the conversation drew to a close, Ramus stared intently at the hooded figure before giving them their final instructions. "Keep an eye on Elara and her entourage," he ordered with an air of authority. "Report back immediately if anything changes or if any new information comes to light."

With a nod of understanding, the hooded figure turned and silently exited Ramus' study, leaving him alone once more with his thoughts.

Chapter 6

The courtyard, once a bustling hub of activity, now lay in ruins. Cracked flagstones and overgrown weeds dominated the desolate expanse, with occasional crumbling statues scattered throughout. The uneven floor testified to the passage of time and neglect. Clutter was strewn about, adding to the eerie atmosphere.

Thane's gaze swept across the decaying hall, taking in the remnants of its former grandeur. Lila's eyes widened in awe as she took in the sight before her. Kael stood thoughtfully, contemplating what this place might have once been.

"This must have been the main hall," Kael mused aloud.

Lila nodded in agreement. "It also looks like a major conflict happened here."

Thane's unease intensified as he sensed a presence beyond his companions. Something wasn't right. He raised his hand and drew his sword, preparing for whatever danger lurked within these walls.

"Everyone," Thane cautioned, "prepare yourselves. We are not alone here."

No sooner had Thane issued his warning than three doors burst open simultaneously—a trio of orcs emerged from within.

"Ah! Humans!" one of them exclaimed with a toothy grin.

The largest orc brandished its rusty blade menacingly at Thane. "Go back! This is Thunderstrike's domain! Surrender or we will make you our tasty dinner!"

Thane muttered under his breath, scowling at their presence. "Orcs! I hate orcs!"

Lila smirked defiantly at their taunts while drawing her daggers—an unmistakable sign that she was ready for battle.

The orcs charged forward recklessly, but Thane met their onslaught with unmatched fury and skill.

As Thane parried the clumsy swing of one orc while delivering a powerful punch to another's face, the third orc swiftly made its way towards a nearby wall. Pulling a rope tied to a metal rung embedded within the stone, the orc triggered a trap.

A net suspended from the ceiling came crashing down, burying Elara and Kael beneath a mound of debris. Their ability to cast supporting magic was thwarted by this unfortunate turn of events.

"Kael!" Lila screamed in alarm as she witnessed her companion being buried under the weight of rocks and wood.

Meanwhile, Thane continued his relentless assault on the orcs, dispatching them with lethal precision.

"Lila! Check on both of them! I'll handle these orcs!" Thane commanded, his voice filled with determination as he continued his assault.

Lila's movements were swift and graceful as she hurried to aid Kael and Elara. She found Kael dazed but unharmed, while Elara emerged from the rubble with some effort.

"Elara, are you alright?" Lila asked anxiously.

"Yes, I think so," Elara replied, her eyes widening suddenly. "Lila! Behind you!"

Lila turned just in time to evade an orc swinging its axe at her. With nimble agility, she dodged its attack as the axe missed its mark and embedded itself into the ground instead.

A surge of adrenaline coursed through Lila's veins as she seized this opportunity. Moving swiftly behind the orc, she plunged both her daggers into its back—ending its life abruptly with a single strike. The orc let out a final scream before collapsing lifelessly to the ground.

Thane's gaze shifted towards Lila's triumph over her opponent; he nodded approvingly. "Nice work."

Returning her attention to Kael, worry etched into her features, Lila asked urgently, "Please tell me you're okay."

Kael accepted Lila's assistance in getting back on his feet. "I will recover, Lila. Just a few bruises."

As Thane helped Elara from the debris, the four companions regrouped and assessed their predicament.

"Now what?" Thane sighed in frustration. "We have three doors to choose from."

Lila, her ears attuned to a faint hissing sound, made her way towards the east door. "I think I heard something. It could be a snake, but it's hard to tell."

Thane stepped forward confidently, gripping his two-handed sword tightly. "Stand back, Lila. If it is a reptile of some sort, I'll put it back in the ground where it belongs."

Thane pushed open the door. As Thane's eyes adjusted to the room's dim lighting, he was greeted with a sight that would haunt his nightmares. The once hallowed room now exuded an air of darkness and despair. Twisted frescoes adorned the walls, depicting unspeakable rituals and ancient evils. The stench of decay and corruption hung heavily in the air. At the heart of the room stood a black stone altar, its surface etched with pulsating ancient runes, radiating malevolent energy. Surrounding the altar were candles burning with an eerie green flame, casting flickering shadows on the walls as they danced in syncopation with the darkness. Above the altar loomed a grotesque icon depicting a twisted deity whose eyes burned with otherworldly fire. The presence of this altar seemed to drain light from the world itself, leaving behind an oppressive sense of dread and foreboding.

A voice emerged from behind the altar, sending shivers down Thane's spine. "Sssso, you have come to ssssurrender your livessss. How ssssad," hissed a tall figure cloaked in darkness.

Lila's eyes widened as she took in what lay before them. "What is that?!" she exclaimed.

Kael too was taken aback by what he saw. "A lizard-man shaman! I never thought such creatures still existed!"

Thane nodded grimly. "Seems like I was right after all; we're dealing with a cold-blooded reptile."

The shaman's scaled skin shimmered like wet stone under the dim light, his eyes glowing with an unnerving malevolence. His long fingers ended in razor-sharp claws while his tail thrashed like a living whip as he chanted words that crawled under their skin like insects. A necklace adorned with human skulls clinked ominously around his neck, and his staff, adorned with feathers and bones, seemed to resonate with dark power. His mere presence seemed to suck the air out of the room, leaving behind a vacuum of evil intent. As he raised his hands towards the sky, shadows writhed and twisted around him, as if the darkness itself were alive and responding to his call.

Suddenly, the lizard-man pointed his sword at Thane and uttered unintelligible words. Fear gripped Thane's heart as he found himself frozen in place, trembling uncontrollably.

Recognizing that her beloved knight was under a fear curse, Elara quickly uttered a prayer in hopes that her faith would dispel his fear.

Realizing it was their chance to strike while the shaman was distracted by Thane's fear-ridden state, Lila sprang into action. She silently moved along the shadows towards the rear of the lizard-man.

Sensing her presence through some sinister intuition, the shaman turned his gaze upon Lila just as she attempted to stab him from behind. With lightning speed, he swiped his hand at her, sending her crashing against the wall with a resounding thud.

Lila clutched her abdomen in pain as she felt an intense burning sensation inside her. Blood trickled down from her nose onto her arm. She knew something was terribly wrong.

Closing in on Lila menacingly with raised sword ready for a fatal strike on this helpless rogue figure before him, a bolt of light slammed into his face blinding him momentarily.

Rubbing his eyes in confusion and pain from this unexpected attack; The shaman growled angrily "What issss thissss!?"

Fully recovered from the fear spell that had paralyzed him moments ago; Thane seized this opportunity to confront their adversary head-on. "That's just a little gift from our wizard friend!" he shouted defiantly. "Now it's time for you to return to the depths of hell where you belong!"

Thane swung his sword with precision and force, knocking the lizard-man's weapon out of his hand. In one swift motion, he brought down his sword, piercing deep into the shaman's chest. The creature crumpled to the ground lifeless.

Kael and Elara rushed to Lila's side as blood continued to flow from her nose, mouth, ears, and every orifice imaginable. She coughed violently and gagged in an attempt to breathe.

The wizard looked on with despair evident on his face. "Is there anything you can do for her, priestess?"

Elara shook her head solemnly. "It looks grim. Battling off that fear spell drained me completely; I'm afraid I don't have enough strength left."

Still hopeful, Elara gently placed her hands on Lila once more and began praying fervently. Beads of sweat formed on her forehead as she poured all her remaining energy into healing Lila. Suddenly, Elara's hands began to glow with a radiant light.

Lila's bleeding slowed down until it ceased entirely. It was as if the blood was evaporating from her face before their very eyes. After a few agonizing minutes, Lila took a deep breath and opened her eyes.

Confusion turned into relief as Lila sat up and looked around at her companions with wonderment in her eyes. "What happened?" she asked in disbelief.

A smile spread across Kael's face as he replied, "How do you feel?"

Lila returned the smile with gratitude in her voice. "Perfectly fine! In fact, I've never felt better in my life!"

Thane interjected pragmatically amidst their rejoicing: "Well then if there are no objections," he said determinedly while gesturing towards the exit of this treacherous lair, "I suggest we keep moving."

Chapter 7

As the adventurers cautiously moved down a short hallway, they came across another door. A flicker of light could be seen underneath the crease of the door, catching their attention. They exchanged uncertain glances before hearing the sound of a whip cracking on the other side. The four adventurers looked at each other, sensing trouble.

Lila swiftly moved to the door, placing her ear against it and listening intently. The crack of the whip grew louder, accompanied by voices emanating from inside. A gravely voice spoke menacingly, "Tell us where the shard is, or we'll teach you the real meaning of suffering!"

"Never!" responded a weak but defiant voice. "You can do whatever you want with me, but I will tell you nothing!"

A second gruff voice chimed in, "This human apparently doesn't know anything."

"You're probably right," replied the first voice dismissively. "But you don't have to spoil my fun."

The defiant voice yelled again with unwavering determination, "Do whatever you want, vile creatures! You will not get a word from me!"

Lila looked back at Kael with wide-eyed surprise and urgency in her expression. "Kael! It sounds like Ferrish! If it's him, he's in trouble!"

Thane drew his two-handed sword upon hearing another crack of the whip. He turned to Lila and commanded firmly, "Stand back!" With all his might, Thane smashed down on the door with his leg. As it flew open abruptly and forcefully startle three hobgoblins within.

"Prepare to feel the pain you so easily inflict upon others now!" Thane bellowed fiercely.

One of the hobgoblins stepped forward brandishing a hot poker and taunted Thane mocking his words saying: "Proud words Knight! Now back them up with steel!"

Without hesitation, Thane engaged the three hobgoblins with the ferocity of a lion. Elara, Lila, and Kael swiftly entered the room and witnessed the intense battle. To their astonishment, they saw Farrish, the missing priest, chained to the back wall. The three adventurers hurriedly made their way toward him.

"Stay back, friends," warned Farrish weakly. "Do not add your deaths to mine!"

Lila looked at Thane with determination and joined in on the fight against the hobgoblins.

Farrish's eyes widened as he locked gazes with Elara. "Elara! Is that you?"

With a calm voice filled with warmth and relief, Elara responded, "Yes, dear friend. It is me."

Kael silently approached Farrish and placed his hands on his manacles. As he focused his energy into them, a faint green aura enveloped them before they snapped apart and fell to the ground effortlessly.

Farrish expressed gratitude toward Kael. "Thank you, kind sir."

Elara turned her attention towards Thane as she witnessed Thane pulling his sword out from one of the fallen hobgoblins while Lila's dagger was lodged perfectly between the eyes of another hobgoblin causing it to fall lifeless to the ground. The third hobgoblin already slain.

Thane and Lila joined them by Farrish's side while catching their breaths after defeating their adversaries.

"You are still as deadly with those blades as you have ever been, Lila," Farrish said warmly with a smile.

Lila embraced Farrish tightly in a hug filled with relief. "I thought you were dead! Your sister asked me to come looking for you."

A flicker of sadness appeared in Farrish's smile before fading away. "I am sorry... I left home over a year ago to work for the church. I have been so busy with my duties that I have had no time to communicate with anyone. Bless High Elder Ramus for sending you, Elara. I thought I would never see anyone again."

Elara placed a delicate hand on Farrish's shoulder, offering comfort. "It's all right now. The High Elder said he sent you here to find a shard."

Farrish's demeanor shifted, becoming more animated with newfound purpose. "Ever since I had a vision of the Holy Stone shards, I began researching their histories and legends. When I requested additional information from High Elder Ramus, he believed he knew where one of the shards would be located."

"He sent me here with a knight and said this castle was abandoned," Farrish continued, frustration seeping into his voice. "I guess he was wrong."

Curiosity piqued within Lila as she asked, "So what happened to you?"

Farrish let out a heavy sigh before recounting his ordeal. "We were attacked by orcs just outside the castle. They knocked me out and dragged me here. I've been their prisoner ever since... I don't know what happened to the knight who was with me. But there are other prisoners here too—a man and a woman—they bring me food sometimes, but I haven't seen anyone else."

Thane crossed his arms thoughtfully and declared, "I say we get him back to the church first, and then we can come back for the shard."

"No! No!" Farrish panicked at Thane's suggestion. "You have to find the shard before these evil creatures do! It's too dangerous to stay lost in their clutches. Even though my strength has deserted me, I can still guide you through all the possible locations... But beware! There is an ogre named Thunderstrike who keeps wolves as pets while commanding orcs and goblins as well!"

Elara attempted to interrupt with concern in her voice, "Then let me heal you before we go—»

But Farrish cut her off. "No! Save your healing for yourselves. You may need your energy during your search for the shard."

Realizing the urgency in Farrish's words, Elara relented. "Then be still and rest. We will be back for you."

With a grateful nod, Farrish watched as the adventurers departed further into the castle, determined to find the shard and bring an end to the evil that lurked within its walls.

The hooded figure stood before High Elder Ramus, his burning curiosity urging him to ask about the rare and mysterious shard. "High Elder, you mentioned a shard... Which shard?" he inquired.

Ramus flashed a mischievous grin and cast a sideways glance at the figure. "Why so interested? No matter. Once I possess the shard, I will create a better world, with myself as its ruler, of course."

Legend spoke of the first shard's ability to control the fabric of space itself. Ramus settled back into his chair behind his desk, intertwining his fingers as he fixed his gaze upon the hooded figure. "The most prominent aspect of this particular shard is its power for teleportation," he began explaining. "Though its range is limited unless it willingly cooperates with its owner."

"Moreover," Ramus continued, "the possessor of this shard can use it to teleport others as well, limited only by their imagination."

"Additionally," he emphasized, "the wielder can manipulate space itself and even simulate gravity's force."

"A fascinating defensive mechanism granted by this shard is the ability to envelop oneself in an ever-shifting warp of space," Ramus elaborated further.

"By manipulating our bodily makeup through altering space proportions," he explained excitedly, "the wielder gains either shrinking or growth abilities."

"And that's not all," Ramus continued enthusiastically. "This marvelous artifact allows its possessor to traverse different planes of existence. Instead of mere teleportation, one can enhance existing forms of travel by boosting their speed."

A wicked smile played on Ramus's lips as he reveled in his plans for ultimate power. "With just this one shard alone, I could create a utopia—a paradise," he mused aloud. "But when all six are united with the Holy Stone... then I shall ascend to the realm of the gods!"

Ramus suddenly caught himself, his overzealous attitude momentarily reined in. "Apologies for my rambling. Enough talk," he declared, resuming his seat. "Send me regular updates and remember to keep our discussion strictly confidential."

The hooded figure nodded respectfully. "As you wish, High Elder."

As the figure closed the door behind him, Ramus rose from his chair and strolled towards the window. Gazing across the horizon, he whispered to himself, "All of this will be mine."

In that moment, the power of the shards filled Ramus's mind with grand visions of a world reshaped according to his desires. With each new revelation about their capabilities, his thirst for dominance grew stronger.

The four adventurers, their torches casting flickering shadows on the damp walls, continued down the narrowing passageway. Elara couldn't help but feel a pang of sorrow for leaving Farrish behind, alone and weakened. "I just hate the thought of him being there all by himself," she expressed her concern to Lila.

Lila responded with a comforting voice, assuring Elara that Farrish was perfectly capable of taking care of himself. "Don't you worry about him. I've known him for a long time. He's resilient," Lila said softly.

Elara smiled gratefully at her friend's reassurance. However, their progress was interrupted as something caught Lila's attention. She motioned for the group to stop and announced her intention to investigate further.

Slowly and cautiously, Lila made her way forward until she reached another oaken door. Putting her ear against it, she could hear the sound of running water from inside. With careful precision, she opened the door and called out to her friends to witness what lay beyond.

Before them stood a breathtaking scene—a courtyard bathed in dappled sunlight within the heart of the forgotten castle. Centuries had etched their secrets into the stone walls that surrounded them, creating an atmosphere thick with history.

In the center of the courtyard stood a weathered yet graceful fountain carved from gray limestone. The scars left by battles long past adorned its surface—chips and grooves telling tales of knights seeking respite and lovers whispering promises. Clear water still flowed from its ornate structure.

The ground beneath their feet was a patchwork quilt of worn cobblestones that seemed to echo footsteps from ages gone by. Moss and tiny wildflowers found refuge in between these stones, softening their harsh lines.

Without hesitation, Kael waved his hand over the water and declared it safe to drink. "We can rest here momentarily," he announced, and the rejuvenating effects of the fountain were felt by all as they drank from its waters.

After a brief respite, Thane surveyed their surroundings, searching for clues on which way to proceed. Disappointed by the lack of obvious signs, he let out a sigh of frustration. It was then that Lila's attention was drawn elsewhere, her senses picking up on something unusual.

Thane approached her cautiously. "Lila, what is it?" he asked, readying himself for any potential threat.

Lila hissed at him to be quiet and held up her hand in warning. She slowly withdrew her two daggers from their sheaths and backed away slowly, keeping her focus on one of the entrances.

"I hear it too," whispered Kael. "It sounds like an animal."

To everyone's surprise, two enormous wolves entered the courtyard with bared teeth and drooling saliva. Thane swiftly drew his sword and positioned himself between the wolves and his companions. But before he could react further, a knife whizzed past him and struck one of the beasts dead.

The second wolf hesitated for a moment before cautiously advancing towards them. As tension filled the air, Kael raised his staff and began chanting a spell while the jewel at its tip shimmered with a green aura.

"Creature of nature, animal of lore," Kael chanted. "Leave in peace and bother us no more!"

The wolves' eyes began to shimmer with the same green aura as it turned tail without making a sound, retreating down the corridor they had come from.

Elara couldn't help but marvel at Kael's magic once again. "That's some skill you have there," she said in awe.

Kael bowed graciously in response to Elara's compliment before their attention was drawn to a rumbling voice coming from another hallway. "Where is my dinner? I'm hungry!" the voice boomed.

Thane put a reassuring hand on Lila's shoulder and took charge of the situation. "Since there doesn't seem to be any hidden threats, I'll take the lead. Lila, stay in the shadows and strike when you get an opportunity. Elara, Kael, stay behind me and be prepared to defend."

As they approached the entranceway where the voice was coming from, Elara began to pray fervently while Thane felt a newfound courage welling up within him.

Upon entering the room, Thane was taken aback by the immense size of an ogre sitting atop a pile of bones with a massive club by its side. The creature stood at least nine feet tall and was covered in matted fur with grotesque features.

Without wasting any time, Thane confronted the ogre boldly. "Sorry to interrupt your precious mealtime," he declared, "but your evil ends now!"

The ogre roared in response, demanding to know who had dared disturb its den of death and destruction. As it searched for something among its belongings in frustration, Lila couldn't resist taunting it about one of its fallen pets.

Enraged by Lila's words, the ogre charged at Thane with its club raised high. But before it could strike him down, Kael created a force field that repelled the attack just inches away from Thane's sword.

Furious at this turn of events, the ogre stepped back momentarily as Thane seized his opportunity to counterattack. With a powerful swing of his sword aimed at Thunderstrike's abdomen but blocked by its club again—Thane managed to deliver a devastating blow using his hilt directly into Thunderstrike's face.

Despite being momentarily stunned by this unexpected hit, Thunderstrike retaliated fiercely by striking back with all its might. Thane was sent flying across the room, crashing into the far wall. The ogre laughed triumphantly, thinking it had won.

Elara screamed in horror at the sight of Thane lying on the ground. But in that moment of despair, she found strength within herself and called upon her faith for divine intervention.

"Blessed Creator," Elara prayed desperately, "please hear your servant's request! Give your Holy Knight the power to defeat this evil!"

In response to her fervent plea, Elara was enveloped in a brilliant light blue aura—a sign that her prayer had been answered. With renewed strength flowing through her, she directed Thane to lift his sword towards the heavens.

Thane felt a surge of energy coursing through him as he raised his sword high. It began to glow brightly, filling him with both peace and strength.

With unwavering determination, Thane charged at Thunderstrike once more. His sword impaled the ogre through its abdomen—a blow that left it clutching its stomach in agony and unable to remove Thane's sword due to its sheer size and weight.

As Thunderstrike lay defeated on the ground, Thane attempted to retrieve his beloved sword from its body but quickly realized it was futile. He sighed in resignation as Elara rushed over to him with open arms.

"Don't worry, Thane," Elara said reassuringly while embracing him tightly. "We can find you another weapon. I'm just glad you're safe."

Thane smiled gratefully at Elara's words but couldn't help but feel a pang of loss for his trusty sword that had served him faithfully for years. Yet Lila interrupted their moment by pointing out something unexpected—on a wooden stand nearby were gleaming artifacts: chain mail armor adorned with an eagle and a shield bearing the same symbol, along with a beautiful large sword reflecting the surrounding light like a beacon.

Kael explained that he had detected magical properties in these artifacts and suggested they bring them back to Farrish for further examination. Elara's excitement was palpable as she urged Thane to try on the armor.

To his surprise, Thane found the new armor to be lighter and more flexible than his previous suit. It fit him like a second skin, offering both comfort and protection. With a newfound sense of confidence, he equipped himself with the shield and sword while Lila rummaged through Thunderstrike's belongings.

Lila's search yielded an intriguing object—a key with holes resembling those of a reed instrument. She suggested trying it out immediately by blowing into it, but Kael advised caution and agreed with Elara that it would be best to consult Farrish first.

Ignoring their cautious advice, Lila couldn't resist a mischievous grin. "Where's the fun in waiting?" she quipped before they set off toward Farrish with their newfound treasures and unanswered questions.

Chapter 8

The companions finally reached Farrish's cell, finding him sitting on a chair next to the crackling fire. As the sound of their footsteps reached his ears, he stood up with an eager look in his eyes.

After exchanging greetings, Kael presented Farrish with the object they had taken from the ogre's belt and held it out in his open hand. "Is this what you were searching for?" he asked.

Farrish's face lit up with a wide smile as he took hold of the item. "Oh, well done, my friends," he exclaimed. "We can thank the Ancient of Days that Thunderstrike was too foolish to blow on it."

With anticipation building in his voice, Farrish raised the object to his lips. "Now, listen."

As he blew gently on the key, a series of five distinct notes filled the air. In response, ethereal voices of angels echoed in harmony, repeating those very same notes from a distance.

Lila's eyes widened at the enchanting sound that surrounded them. "What was that?" she asked in awe.

Farrish looked at her with a triumphant expression as if he had just solved a great riddle. "That," he declared proudly, "was the song of the shard. The music called out to it and awakened its presence."

Thane spoke up curiously. "It sounded as though it came from nearby," he observed.

Farrish nodded enthusiastically. "Indeed it did! You must go to the adjacent rooms and use this key to unlock the door concealing the shard."

Eagerly retrieving the key from Farrish's grasp, Kael led his companions forward once again in search of this elusive magical door.

The group navigated through dimly lit corridors and winding passageways until they reached a dead end.

With a deep breath, Kael blew into the key and the song answered. A small keyhole appeared, and Kael inserted the key into the lock and turned it slowly. The wall magically separated open revealing a small chamber bathed in soft golden light. In the center of the room stood a pedestal upon which rested the coveted shard.

Its brilliance was mesmerizing—a translucent crystal pulsating with an otherworldly glow. As Lila approached, she could feel its power resonating within her being.

Thane stepped forward cautiously, his eyes fixed on the shard. "Is this what we've been searching for all along?" he wondered aloud.

Kael reached out to touch the shard, feeling a tingling sensation coursing through his fingertips. He withdrew his hand quickly as if burned by its intensity.

"We must be careful," he warned his companions. "Such raw power can be both a blessing and a curse."

Lila's gaze never wavered from the radiant crystal before them. "But think of what we could accomplish with this," she said dreamily. "Imagine all the good we could do."

Thane's voice held a hint of skepticism as he spoke up once more. "And what if this power falls into the wrong hands? What if it brings only destruction?"

As they stood there, contemplating their newfound responsibility, a sudden gust of wind blew through the chamber, extinguishing all torches but one—an omen perhaps or simply nature's way of reminding them of the delicate balance between light and darkness.

The companions reached a silent agreement. They would protect the shard, not just for their own sake but for the sake of all those who depended on them. They would return the shard to Valoria so the church could properly protect the shard.

Suddenly, Thane's sword began to glow with a golden aura and hum with a dull resonance. Kael's eyes grew wide. "Knight, look at your sword!"

Elara held onto her staff tighter. "Something is very wrong here. Brace yourselves, my friends."

Meanwhile, in the chamber of High Elder Ramus, a sense of unease hung heavy in the air. Restless and tormented by his nightmares, Ramus tossed and turned in his bed, unable to find solace in sleep. Visions of ominous imagery plagued his mind, leaving him disoriented and anxious.

In the midst of this turmoil, a deep and haunting voice echoed through the room. "Ramus!"

Startled awake, Ramus sat up abruptly. Sweat dripped down his forehead as he frantically scanned the room for the source of the voice. "Who... who's there?" he stammered.

The voice boomed once again, its tone even more thunderous than before. "Ramus, the time is drawing near!"

Ramus felt a surge of agitation coursing through him. "Where are you? And who are you?" he demanded.

The voice responded with an air of superiority. "You need only know that I am Natas, the great red Dragon who has been observing your progress."

With a mix of trepidation and curiosity gripping him, Ramus swung his legs over the side of his bed and stood up, clutching his robe tightly around himself. "How can I be certain that you are who you claim to be?"

In an instant, a brilliant flash of red lightning illuminated Ramus' chamber. And just as suddenly as it had appeared, it dissipated to reveal a man with fiery red hair and beard standing before him wearing regal robes befitting nobility. The sight took Ramus aback; it was an intrusion unlike any other he had experienced.

The figure lifted its head to meet Ramus' gaze; its eyes burned like molten rock with an intensity that sent shivers down Ramus' spine. "Do I not impress you?" it asked with an edge to its voice.

Ramus crossed his arms defiantly. "It will take more than a mere teleportation spell and theatrical effects to sway me."

Fury and malevolence twisted the nobleman's features. "You dare mock my power?!" he thundered.

Without warning, Natas raised his hands toward the ceiling, conjuring bolts of red lightning that crashed down upon the chamber, causing tiny fragments of stone to rain down on Ramus. Overwhelmed by fear, Ramus fell to his knees. "I'm sorry! I never meant to question you, mighty Natas. I merely sought confirmation if you were truly the one spoken of in legends!"

"You shall address me as your master," declared Natas with an air of authority. "For I am power incarnate!"

Ramus bowed his head reluctantly, swallowing his pride as he did so. "Yes, master."

Natas' voice grew firmer as he continued to assert dominance over Ramus. "When you acquire the shards, you will deliver them to me without delay. In return for your loyalty and obedience, I shall grant you your deepest desire. Until then, your every action shall be guided by my instructions."

"My most trusted allies are already working towards obtaining the shards for me, my Lord," Ramus responded with a mixture of fear and determination.

"Bring me the shards!" Natas' voice dripped with menace before another surge of red lightning enveloped him once more. And just like that, he vanished into thin air, leaving behind only a lingering scent of brimstone.

Ramus regained his footing and stared at the spot where Natas had disappeared from in disbelief. "When I possess those shards," Ramus muttered under his breath, a newfound resolve in his eyes, "it will be you who addresses me as master."

"Don't be so superstitious, Elara," Lila said, trying to convey a sense of confidence that she herself was struggling to feel.

As soon as she spoke, the torches on the walls flickered to life, burning with a newfound intensity.

Thane tightened his grip on his sword, readying himself for an attack from an unknown enemy. "Elara! The torches lit up on their own and, if you haven't noticed, they're casting some strange shadows."

Kael also held his staff firmly. "You're right in your observation, knight. The shadows are taking shape."

Before the companions' startled eyes, the flickering shadows transformed into beastly forms. Menacing yellow eyes materialized within them and the air itself seemed to ripple and distort as if reality was warping under its presence. The shadow pulsated with a malevolent energy, waiting for the perfect moment to strike. Its edges blurred into the surrounding darkness like an insidious stain spreading across the walls.

In a swift motion akin to a flickering candle's dance, one of the shadows lunged at Lila before she could even draw her weapons.

The shadow's clawed hand tore through Lila's sleeve on her upper right arm. As she fell to the ground clutching her wounded arm, uncontrollable shivers racked her body. "Cold! So cold! Get them away from me!"

Thane immediately positioned himself between Lila and the shadows. "Alright you foul beast! If it's a fight you seek!"

Thane's sword glowed with magnificent brilliance that kept the shadows at bay for now. But he knew it wouldn't last forever.

Elara stood by Thane's side as her most trusted protector and fervently prayed for their safety. Her staff illuminated alongside Thane's sword.

Lifting her head weakly from where she lay, Lila looked at her wizard companion. "Kael! You must do something!"

Deep in thought, Kael raised his staff and began whispering secret incantations. A gentle breeze brushed against their skin.

Then he pointed his staff towards the shadows and a powerful gust of wind surged past them, extinguishing the two torches. As the lights vanished, so did the shadows with a haunting moan.

Lila slowly rose from the ground, brushing dirt off her leggings. "I knew you could do it, Kael!"

Elara relaxed her grip on her staff as Thane sheathed his sword, its glow fading back to normal. She turned to Kael. "How did you know that extinguishing the torches would save us?"

"It was simple logic," Kael replied confidently. "I noticed that the shadows were responding to light. By extinguishing the flames and plunging us into darkness, we eliminated their source of shadow creation. These were no ordinary elements we faced."

Thane surveyed their surroundings anxiously. "That's why it's crucial for us to get this shard to safety. I don't want to overstay our welcome here."

Elara retrieved a small sack from her belt and carefully covered the shard inside before securing it firmly. "You're right, Thane. Our mission will be complete once we deliver this shard safely. Let's regroup with Farrish and ensure he returns home unharmed as well."

With no further need for discussion or explanation, the companions hurriedly made their way out of the room.

Breathing heavily as they emerged into a dimly lit corridor, Thane glanced back at Lila's wounded arm with concern etched on his face.

Lila reassured him with a faint smile despite her pain. "I'll be alright, Thane."

Thane nodded solemnly before leading them forward once more.

Chapter 9

The morning sun cast a warm glow over the grand halls of the church of Valoria. High Elder Ramus, still in his night robes, was abruptly awakened by a knock on his chamber door. Startled, he stumbled out of bed and hurriedly made his way to answer the call.

"High Elder! Are you awake?" came a voice from behind the wooden doors.

Ramus paused for a moment to collect himself before responding. "Yes! Yes, what is it!" he exclaimed with irritation evident in his voice.

The doors swung open abruptly, revealing a hooded figure standing before him. Ramus squinted through disheveled hair to get a better look. "Who are you? What do you want?" he demanded, clearly annoyed at being disturbed.

The figure took a step back at Ramus' agitated state but maintained composure as he spoke. "Your Excellency, High Priestess Elara has arrived with her knight and companions," he explained calmly. "She is currently speaking with High Elder Vian. It seems they have completed their mission."

Ramus stood frozen for a moment as shock coursed through him. "What?!" he exclaimed in disbelief. "Why wasn't I notified of their arrival?"

The hooded figure kept his calm demeanor and replied without hesitation, "High Elder Vian ordered us not to disturb you. I tried to inform you as soon as I could."

Enraged by this revelation, Ramus glared at the hooded figure before him. His anger boiled over as he shouted, "Leave me! I'll deal with you later!"

Without uttering another word, Ramus slammed the door shut and hastily dressed himself in an attempt to make himself presentable before joining the other elders.

High Elder Vian stood proudly and regally in his white and purple robes, addressing the four companions in the serene garden. A gentle breeze carried the scent of honeysuckle through the air as he began to speak.

"Well done, brave heroes. You have successfully carried out your mission and saved Farrish's life," Vian spoke with pride. "I am incredibly proud of each and every one of you. Your actions have made our land safe once again, not just for our city but also for the surrounding kingdoms."

Elara bowed respectfully. "It was an honor to serve."

Kael, the wizard among them, inquired about the fate of the shard they had retrieved. "What will become of the shard?"

Vian's gaze fixed on Kael as he responded. "The shard will be securely kept by our holy guards, where only myself and the most high elder will know its location. These objects possess great power and must not be handled carelessly."

Elara looked puzzled as she posed another question. "What about High Elder Ramus? After all, he was the one who sent us on this mission."

A slight chuckle escaped Vian's lips before he replied, "Actually, I provided Ramus with those orders to pass on to you. I knew that you would be the only ones I could trust to complete this delicate task successfully. As for Ramus himself, he has his own agenda and will remain unaware of where these holy objects are being safeguarded."

Before any further questions could be raised by their curious minds, Vian concluded with a final statement. "Once again, I cannot express enough gratitude for a job well done. And should there come a time when your services are needed again, may I count on each of you?"

With that said, High Elder Vian turned away from them and began making his way towards the council chambers. Lila, the ever-curious rogue, couldn't help but express his curiosity. "I wonder what kind of conversation will unfold between Vian and Ramus."

Elara turned to face Kael and Lila, expressing her heartfelt appreciation. "I would like to extend my deepest gratitude to both of you for your unwavering support throughout all of this."

Kael smiled warmly. "There is no need for thanks, dear priestess. We are all inhabitants of this land and what we were involved in affected our entire realm. If we had chosen not to act, we would have surely faced dire consequences."

Lila chimed in playfully, "Come on, Kael. Let's go celebrate with a drink."

Agreeing with a nod, Kael and Lila set off towards the 'Tavern of the Morning Star'. As they disappeared from sight, Elara turned her attention to Thane.

"Do you think we will be able to find the other shards within our lifetime?" Elara asked with a glimmer of hope in her eyes.

Thane's smile was filled with reassurance as he responded gently. "That is entirely up to the will of the Ancient of Days'. It seems that you hold a special place within His plan. All we can do is have patience and trust that everything will unfold as it should."

Elara reached out and took Thane's hand in hers, grateful for his wisdom and guidance throughout their journey together.

"I believe you are right, Thane," she said softly. "Thank you once again for your unwavering support and counsel."

Thane squeezed her hand reassuringly and smiled warmly at her. "Know this: wherever duty calls or whatever lies ahead for you, I will always be right by your side."

www.ingramcontent.com/pod-product-compliance
Lightning Source LLC
Chambersburg PA
CBHW031553310726
48973CB00003B/813